CONCORD PIKE LIBY
3406 CONCORD PIKE
WILMINGTON, DE 19803

03/02/1999   206036797

P9-BBP-774

Canoe Days

Canoe Days

Gary Paulsen

Illustrated by
Ruth Wright Paulsen

DOUBLEDAY

A DOUBLEDAY BOOK FOR YOUNG READERS

Published by
Bantam Doubleday Dell Publishing Group, Inc.
1540 Broadway, New York, New York 10036

Text copyright © 1999 by Gary Paulsen
Illustrations copyright © 1999 by Ruth Wright Paulsen
Doubleday and the portrayal of an anchor with a dolphin are trademarks of
Bantam Doubleday Dell Publishing Group, Inc.
All rights reserved. No part of this book may be reproduced or transmitted in any form or by any means, electronic or
mechanical, including photocopying, recording, or by any information storage and retrieval system, without the written
permission of the Publisher, except where permitted by law.

Library of Congress Cataloging-in-Publication Data
Paulsen, Gary.
Canoe days / Gary Paulsen ; illustrated by Ruth Wright Paulsen.
p.   cm.
Summary: A canoe ride on a northern lake during a summer day reveals the quiet beauty
and wonder of nature in and around the peaceful water.
ISBN 0-385-32524-X
[1. Nature—Fiction. 2. Summer—Fiction.] I. Paulsen, Ruth Wright, ill. II. Title.
PZ7. P2843Ca ln 1998
[E]—dc21   97-21542
                                                                          CIP
                                                                          AC

The text of this book is set in 27-point Tempus Sans .
Book design by Semadar Megged
Manufactured in the United States of America
April 1999
10 9 8 7 6 5 4 3 2 1

For
Ruth Ann *and* Don Nordlund

Sometimes when it is still,
so still you can hear the swish
of a butterfly's wing—

sometimes when it is that still I take the canoe
out on the edge of the lake.

One stroke of the paddle and we are gone, the canoe and me, moving silently.

Across water so quiet it becomes part of the sky, the canoe slides in green magic without a ripple,

disappears like a ghost floating in the
airwater over the playground where fish play.

The water is a window into the skylake.

Sunfish under lily pads living in cool green rooms, watching for water bugs to make a lunch. Watching for frogs to make a dinner.

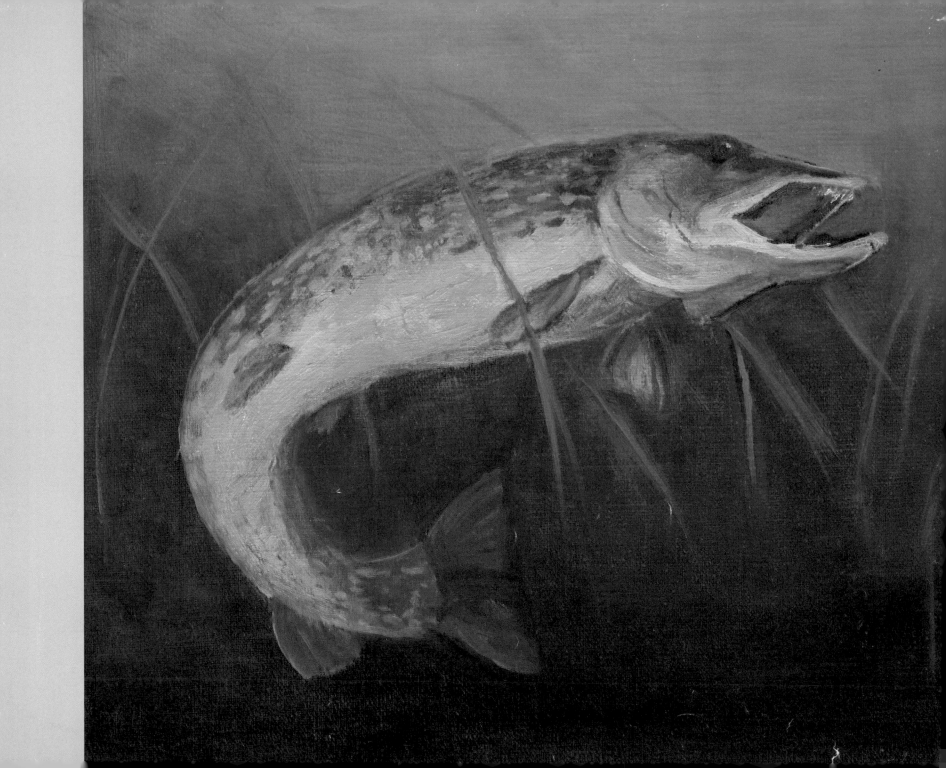

But still now, everything frozen while the
cold slash of a hunting northern pike moves
like an arrow through the pads, looking, fiercely
searching always for something to eat; and then
he's gone into the green depths.

Ahead is a mallard hen, her ducklings spread out like a spotted fan around her looking for skittering oar bugs to eat. The canoe does not frighten her—she does not see the man, only the canoe, as a shiny log floating in the sun.

And there a fawn, on the edge, his feet in the water, ears flopping the flies away while he watches the canoe glide past, as unafraid as the mallard.

But his mother is near, in the bush, knowing better and trying to get him away with short stamps of her feet.

Come away now. Come away *now*.

A fox drinks, soft laps with a pink tongue while the paddle waits, all still. Then the fox slips away.

A raccoon turns a log looking for worms to eat.

A snake moves from
shore to pad, a wavy ripple, green back and
light belly making it invisible when it stops.

And then, perfect on the brim of my
cap, a dragonfly catches a deerfly that would
have bitten me and eats there without leaving;

while I hold my breath and see the fawn and the
ducks and the doe and the snake and the frogs
and the fish and the fox and the badger all
around me while the sun is on my back like a
golden friend on this perfect day.

A canoe day.